Hot on the Scent

For a free color catalog describing Gareth Stevens' list of high-quality books,
call 1-800-341-3569 (USA) or 1-800-461-9120 (Canada).

Library of Congress Cataloging-in-Publication Data

Bech, Bente.
 [Duften i luften. English]
  Hot on the scent / pictures by Bente Bech ; story [idea] by Peter Lind.
    p. cm.
  Translation of: Duften i luften.
  Summary: Following an enticing smell, a mouse braves many dangers to
reach his destination.
  ISBN 0-8368-0510-0
  [1. Mice—Fiction. 2. Stories without words.] I. Title.
PZ7.B38065Ho 1992
 [E]—dc20   92-8782

North American edition first published in 1992 by
Gareth Stevens Publishing
1555 North RiverCenter Drive, Suite 201
Milwaukee, WI 53212, USA

Hot on the Scent

Pictures by Bente Bech
Story by Peter Lind

Gareth Stevens Publishing
MILWAUKEE